KU-741-692

Callum McCoodle

By Jenny Oldfield
illustrated by Ella Oxstad

Contents

PEARSON Longman

PEARSON EDUCATION LIMITED
Edinburgh Gate
Harlow
Essex CM20 2JE
England

www.longman.co.uk

First published 2004
ISBN 0582 79639 3

Illustrated by Ella Oxstad (The Organisation)

Printed in Great Britain by Scotprint, Haddington

The publishers' policy is to use paper manufactured from sustainable forests.

1 Asking For Trouble!

From the start Callum McCoodle reckoned that it was asking for trouble.

"How can anyone in their right mind let us lot loose on a farm?" he asked. "I mean, they've got pigs and pig muck, cows and cow muck, sheep and sheep ..."

But that was exactly what their teacher, Miss Hallam, had decided to do. "I'm taking 7JH to Low Hall Farm," she'd announced in the staffroom at the start of the summer term. "I think it will be good for these city children to see where their milk and food come from!"

"Fat lot of good that'll do!" Mr Baxter had snorted.

"Isn't a farm a rather dangerous place for the likes of Callum and Zeta?" Mrs Truman had clucked.

"... muck!" Callum went on as he climbed into the bus. "Horse muck and hen muck ..."

"Get a move on, Callum MuckCoodle!" Zeta Davies shoved him up the top step. She slung her sandwich box onto the rack above her head. Then she bagged the seat next to her for her best friend, Zoey Boot.

Callum glared over his shoulder. "No need to get your knickers in a twist," he told Zeta. The back seat was for him and Shane.

Gradually the bus filled up. Miss Hallam, helped by Naomi's mum, Mrs Wilks, ticked her list, then gave the driver directions to Low Hall.

"I once went to a farm," Shane claimed, stretched out on the back seat, arms behind his head. "I touched a sheep!"

"What happened? Did the poor thing die of fright?" Callum asked, stretched out in the opposite direction.

Rrrr! The driver revved the engine. *Jerk!* He took off the handbrake.

Thump! Callum and Shane rolled onto the floor.

"Sit up straight at the back and fasten your seat belts!" Miss Hallam screeched.

Vroom! The bus set off. *Bump-bump-bump!* A dozen lunch boxes fell off the overhead racks.

"Put all your packed lunches under the seats!" the teacher ordered.

Zeta and Zoey snaffled a stray box and tucked into someone's bacon sandwiches.

"Y'know this bacon comes from a pig, and soon we're gonna see a real live one!" Zoey muttered.

"Oink!" Zeta replied. "Poor pig, but yummy bacon."

"It's weird going to a farm and seeing all these animals," Zoey went on. "I mean, how big is a real live cow, for a start?"

"This big!" Zeta stretched her arms wide.

"Bigger," Mrs Wilks assured her.

"Ha, Zeta-Ryvita doesn't even know the size of a cow!" Callum yelled.

"I meant a baby cow!" Zeta retorted. "You keep your nose out, Callum McCoodle-Doodle!" Then she thought of something that would definitely shut him up. "Hey, maybe we'll see a calf being born, all slimy and slippery, and then the mother cow has to lick it clean. I've seen it on the telly!"

"Yuck gross!" The boys at the back fell sickly silent as, bit by bit, the bus left the streets and shops behind.

* * * * *

"Give me footie any day," Callum sighed, staring out at green fields.

And it's McCoodle going in hard, taking the ball from Brazil's Martinez, bending the ball to the England captain, who scores from well outside the box ...

What exactly was the point of taking them to see boring animals?

"Remember to bring your worksheets with you," Miss Hallam reminded them. "You will need a pencil and something to lean on."

That's 3–0 to England, thanks to superb attacking from McCoodle.

A murmur of disapproval filled the bus. "This is supposed to be a day out. Miss, why do we have to do work?"

"And there are rules for you to follow!" The teacher continued. "First, you must always stay with a partner. Never wander off alone."

At sixteen years and two days, McCoodle is the youngest player ever to achieve an England cap … Callum dreamed of the future.

"Second, no trespassing!" Miss Hallam warned. "Third, be polite at all times. Fourth, don't feed the animals unless a member of the farm staff gives you permission."

"Did you get all that?" Shane asked Callum, holding onto his stomach as the bus swayed down twisty roads.

"Nope."

"Me neither."

At last they turned down a narrow lane and came to a halt beside a sign that read Low Hall Farm.

Miss Hallam saw that she was fast losing the class's attention. "Choose a partner!" the new teacher screeched. She felt very hot and a bit faint.

"Watch out!"

"Miss, he squished my sarnies!"

"Ouch, that was my foot!"

The scrum for the door sent Miss Hallam reeling into the bus driver's arms.

"Rather you than me," the driver said, setting the skinny teacher back on her feet.

She took a deep breath then followed the kids. "Callum, come back here! Zeta, leave Zoey alone!" she wailed.

2 Meet the Animals

Low Hall Farm stood by a pond in front of a river.

Miss Hallam and Mrs Wilks watched in dismay as Zeta and Zoey charged over to feed the ducks on the pond.

"Miss! Shane and Callum have stripped off to the nud and jumped in the river!" Henry Saville reported. "Only kidding!" he added as the teacher rushed to the spot.

The farmhouse was built of stone, with stone barns attached. No longer a working farm, it had opened up as a learning centre, complete with small animals such as chickens and rabbits, through medium ones like sheep, goats and pigs, up to large cows, donkeys and horses.

"Mum, look at the cute little chicks!" Naomi Wilks cried.

Inside the nearest barn, dozens of fluffy yellow

chicks cheeped and pecked at their grain under giant heat lamps.

"Aaaah!" the girls whispered, while the woman in charge let Naomi pick up a five-day-old chick and stroke it.

Then, "Miss, come and see this black rabbit with floppy ears!" Zoey called the teacher into a wooden shed. Inside there were rabbits, guinea pigs, hamsters and ferrets.

"Who wants to take this ferret for a walk?" a man with a badge asked.

Zeta shot forward. "Me!" she said.

She walked the fidgety ferret up and down a stretch of grass outside, holding on tight to its lead.

The man with the badge introduced himself to the teacher. "I'm Pete, the manager round here. If there's anything you want to know, just ask!"

Miss Hallam blushed and giggled.

"He fancies her!" Henry announced, to looks of horror and disbelief.

"No way!"

"You're kidding!"

"Smarmy geezer!"

Meanwhile, Zeta went on walking the ferret. "This is funky. What's its name?" she asked Pete, studying its sleek body, fierce face and long tail.

"It doesn't have a name yet," he replied. "It's just arrived."

Over in the farmyard, another helper herded an enormous pig into a pen.

"Come and meet Miss Piggy," Pete invited, intending to lead the way in his green wellies and knobbly grey sweater.

But Class 7JH were well ahead of him.

"Wow, look at the size of that sucker!" Shane screeched to a halt just short of the metal barrier.

Miss Piggy was pink, smooth and fat as a barrel.

"Wow!" Callum cried. It seemed that Miss Piggy's little legs would snap under her weight.

"Aah Mum, mini pigs!" Naomi cooed, spotting piglets in some straw.

By this time, Zeta had ditched the ferret and sprinted across.

"Back off!" Callum complained as she pinned him against the barrier.

"Muck-Coodle-Doodle, cock-a-doodle-do!" she muttered. "Ah look, the little pigs want their lunch!"

The piglets squirmed and tumbled towards Miss Piggy, who tilted onto her side like the sinking Titanic, then settled into the straw. The piglets squealed with delight and started sucking. Callum and Shane pulled faces and looked away.

"I'm never gonna eat bacon ever again!" Zoey vowed.

"The pigs are the bosses around here!" Pete explained. "You don't get in the way of a pig if you can possibly help it."

Splatted! Squished! Callum pictured the mess if ten tonnes of pig steamrollered you. He was so busy imagining it that he didn't notice a sly pig come up and snaffle his worksheet from his pocket until it was way too late.

"Miss!" he squeaked, leaping away. "The pig ate my worksheet!"

Zeta looked across at Callum. "How sad is that!" she said to Zoey, leading a splinter group away to look at some lambs.

The lambs were in a field behind the pigsties. They leaped and played on their skinny black legs, just like in the picture books.

"They're woolly jumpers!" Henry giggled.

"That's so not funny!" Naomi told him.

Then Miss Hallam decided it was time to get down to some serious work. "Don't forget your worksheets," she bleated.

7JH rushed over to the next field, where two donkeys, five ponies and a goat grazed.

"Meet Daisy and Maxwell!" Pete introduced the donkeys. "The goat is called Gordon, and here are the ponies. Would anyone care for a ride?"

Miss Hallam closed her eyes and held her breath when she saw that Callum McCoodle was the first in the saddle.

The kids had watched patiently as Pete and a stable girl called Hayley brought out the saddles, hats and bridles.

"Whatever you do, don't kick and scream," Pete had warned. "Just sit nice and easy in the saddle and press gently with your heels. And remember, your pony is bigger and stronger than you, so respect her, please!"

"Yee-hah!" Callum had swaggered to the front of the queue, ahead of Zoey and Zeta.

"Ride 'em, cowboy!" Shane drawled as Callum swung his leg over Dolly's saddle.

Dolly looked bored. She was a mottled grey pony with a long white mane and tail.

Callum looked down at the ground. "Wow, this felt high!" He had never liked heights. And when Dolly started to sway and take a step forward he felt his stomach churn with fear. But he wouldn't let the others see it. "Giddy-up!" he yelled, kicking hard with his heels.

Dolly shot forward at a trot – up-down, up-down! Callum bounced. His backside was bruised. "Aah!" he cried. "Ouch! Help, how do I stop?"

"Whoah, Dolly!" Swiftly Hayley stepped up beside the runaway pony. She took hold of the loose reins. Dolly stopped. Callum shot forward over the front of the saddle and landed in a heap.

"Aaagh!" he cried.

"Who's next?" the manager asked, but magically the queue had melted away.

3 The Pig Ate My Worksheet

"The thing is, Callum's thick," Zeta said. There were no two ways about it. You just had to watch him trying to ride a pony to realise that.

Naomi and Zoey giggled in agreement. They laughed at anything Zeta said, and followed wherever she led.

After all, Zeta was a good laugh, and clever with it. Whenever a teacher was about to tell her off, she would give them her best 'Who me?' look.

She would flick her long, dark hair and look up with her big, dark eyes. "Who me, Miss? I don't think so, Miss!"

And the teacher would believe her.

Now Zeta sat astride a hay bale in the barn and tried to wind Callum up. "Boys never listen. They always make out they're Mister Big, when really they're not."

"Zeta and Callum, get on with your worksheets!" Miss Hallam ordered.

"Miss, the pig ate mine!" Callum reminded her. He put on his innocent look, but it was nowhere near as good as Zeta's.

"How many piglets does a sow produce in an average litter?" Naomi read out. "Is it a) 1, b) 50, c) 6, d) 20? Easy-peasy!"

"Callum, get down to work!" the teacher nagged. She and Mrs Wilks had gathered 7JH in a converted barn, which contained a study room and a café. It was only 11.00 a.m. and the teacher was already feeling frazzled.

"Miss, I can't. I haven't got a worksheet. The pig ate it!" Callum insisted.

Miss Hallam tutted. "I've heard some daft excuses, but this one takes the biscuit!"

Talking of biscuits, Callum was famished. "Well, maybe I left my worksheet on the coach," he conceded. "Can I go and look?"

Zeta eyed him suspiciously.

Actually, the pig

had eaten his questionnaire; she'd seen it. "He can share mine, Miss!" she offered, hoping to spoil whatever it was he was about to get up to.

Callum gave her an icy stare. "No, honest Miss – I'll go and fetch it!" Then, without waiting for an answer, he fled.

"Two chocolate bars!" Callum headed straight for the shop to sort out his empty stomach. He was munching happily by the time he was strolling across the farmyard. Ah, this was cool! Sun shining, chicks running here and there, a couple of ducks crossing his path, straw blowing in the breeze ...

"Shouldn't you be in the study room with the others?" Pete asked from inside the pigsty.

Callum stopped dead.

And McCoodle is intercepted by a hefty tackle, which brings him down just outside the penalty area! He appeals to the ref ...

"I lost my worksheet in the field with the horses," he lied. "Miss Hallam told me to go and find it."

Pete nodded. "Okay then. But make sure you don't go upsetting any of the animals." He watched suspiciously as Callum scooted off past the lambs then turned the corner towards the field containing the ponies, donkeys and goat.

McCoodle is back on the attack – there's no stopping the England striker – he weaves through the defence, the goalmouth is open except for the goalie. Bam! The ball's in the back of the net and the crowd are on their feet – it's goal number three for Callum Golden-Boot McCoodle!

Callum grinned to himself as he stopped to survey the horses. Then, because it was bound to be breaking a farm rule, he went right up to the gate, opened it and slipped into the field. He was steering well clear of Dolly the pony though.

A brown pony with a black mane came and nuzzled his arm.

"Gerroff!" Callum muttered, stepping quickly to one side. Right into some horse muck. Yuck!

"Eeee-aw!" The two donkeys brayed, as if

Callum's little mishap was hilarious. They threw back their heads, showed their big flat teeth and laughed.

Disgusted, Callum wiped the side of his trainer on the grass. This stuff would stink the coach out on the way back if he didn't get it off.

Close by, one of the animals snickered.

"Wow!" Callum looked up, right into the staring green eyes of a jet-black goat. The goat had a thin beard and pointed horns. BIG, fat, slightly curved ones. "Get lost!" he told it, in no uncertain terms.

But Gordon the goat didn't take orders. He came close and nibbled at the visitor's pockets. Anything to eat? Chomp! Gordon bit into a chocolate bar, then swallowed it, wrapper and all.

"Hey!" Callum squeaked. "Phuh!" He breathed hard. Those horns looked evil.

Nibble-nibble. Gordon continued with his raid. Nothing else in the other pockets. The boy's hair gel smelled pretty tasty though.

Callum felt the goat's hot breath on his neck. Time to run! Setting off for the gate at a sprint, he squished into more muck, slid and fell headlong.

Gordon snickered and cantered past. No more food on the kid, but he'd left the gate ajar. How careless was that?

Looking up from the ground, Callum watched helplessly as the goat gathered speed and charged for the gate. He groaned to see him butt it wide open then hurtle through.

Freedom! Gordon clattered out of the field and up the path to the farm.

Callum picked himself up and sprinted after the runaway. What kind of trouble would he be in if Pete found out who had left the gate open?

Yeah, that was a major point! Callum wasn't meant to be anywhere near the field in the first place. He was supposed to be fetching his worksheet from the bus.

Hmm, he'd better think this one through …

Okay, this was the plan …

4 Callum Muck-Coodle

"Sorry, Miss, I couldn't find my worksheet on the bus," Callum told Miss Hallam when he sauntered back into the study room, hands in pockets, spiky hair a little flattened by Gordon's steamy breath.

"What? Oh, never mind. Share Henry's," the teacher snapped. She looked at her watch and decided that it was almost time to take the class out on their "Guided Tour, Part Two".

"Pwoah, you stink!" Zeta hissed at Callum as he passed by.

"Yeah, you stink," Shane agreed, glancing down at Callum's stained trainers.

Callum slid onto Shane's bench. "Don't make a big thing of it, okay!" he urged.

"But what is it?" His best mate held his nose and edged away.

"Horse muck."

"Phwaagh!" Shane stifled a loud guffaw.

"Yeah, right. And listen, the goat did a runner!" Callum confessed. "But don't say anything."

"The goat did what?" Shane hissed back.

Callum saw Zeta, Zoey and Naomi looking at him and giggling. "Scarpered!" he muttered. "But the plan is to say nothing, pretend we don't know. Then when someone eventually finds out, we make out, like, 'What goat? What gate?' Like, it's the first we heard of it!"

Shane approved the plan. "If you give me half your sarnies," he bargained.

"That's tight!" Callum moaned, but he was in no position to argue.

"What are you two on about?" Zeta quizzed from across the long table. In spite of the bad pong, she eased herself towards Callum. "You're up to something, aren't you?"

Callum turned up his nose. "Can you smell that?" he asked Shane.

It was always best to turn a bad situation against your enemy.

"I think it's Zeta's perfume!" Shane got in on the joke.

Zeta frowned. "Watch it," she warned. "I know you never went looking for your stupid worksheet, even if Miss doesn't!"

"Prove it!" Callum sneered, all set for a fight.

But just then, Pete walked in. "Hi," he said to Miss Hallam, all bright and breezy.

"H-h-hi!" she stammered back. She looked sideways from under her mousy fringe. "We were just finishing here."

"Yes, I wondered if you'd like to bring your group to watch the blacksmith shoe one of our horses." Pete oozed charm. He came across as rugged and outdoorsy, like there were big muscles lurking under his boring jumper.

"Yeah!" the kids cried, abandoning their sheets and scrambling for the door.

"Phwoah, McCoodle, you stink!" Henry Saville said in passing.

In passing, Callum stood on his toe with his smelly trainer. "Sorry, Hen!" he declared.

"Find your partner, don't run, follow Pete," Miss Hallam ordered with a bright red face.

"So far, so good!" Callum thought. As yet, no one had noticed that Gordon the goat was missing. He grinned at Shane and followed their leader.

"A horse needs new shoes every six weeks on average," Pete explained.

Class 7JH had gathered around the blacksmith's van, standing well back from big old Dolly.

"Horses' hooves grow just like your fingernails," Pete went on, obviously wanting to impress Miss Hallam with his expert knowledge of a horse's beauty regime. "The blacksmith takes off the old shoes, files down the hoof then shapes the new shoes by heating them up."

"Don't the nails hurt when he hammers them in?"

Zeta smelled the scorched hoof and heard it sizzle as the blacksmith fitted a front shoe. "Gross!" Yet Dolly didn't move a muscle.

Callum thought this was the best bit of the day so far. All that yanking nails out and heating up the new shoe was cool. He was so interested he hardly felt Shane's dig in the ribs.

"Mrs Wilks, Naomi feels sick!" Zeta piped up. She was bored with the blacksmith and this was the first feeble excuse that came into her head. "Can I go with her to the toilet?"

"As long as you're quick," Naomi's mum reluctantly agreed. "C'mon!" Zeta pulled her friend out of the crowd and headed for the ladies.

Meanwhile, Callum glanced over his shoulder. "Shane, quit jabbing me, will you?"

Shane's eyes were wide. "Look at that!" he hissed, pointing towards the sky.

"Later!" Callum insisted.

"Each horse's feet are unique," Cheesy Pete explained. "The blacksmith's skill is in shaping the shoe to the foot."

Hiss, sizzle, hammer. Dolly was fitted with shoe number two. Then more yanking and filing for three and four.

"You felt sick, but now you feel loads better," Zeta was explaining to Naomi as they veered off

course around the ladies and nipped into the shop
for supplies of crisps. They chomped their way
through the snack then stuck some money in the
machine for two ice-cold drinks.

Naomi giggled, leading the way out of the
shop. Then she stopped short on the step. "Whoa,
am I seeing things, or what?"

"What?" Zeta asked. She looked along the
barn roof where her friend had pointed but saw
nothing.

Naomi rubbed her eyes. "Nah, it couldn't
be ..."

Zeta looked again. "Couldn't be what?"

"They can't ... can they?"

"Can't what?" By now Zeta was getting mad.
She stared at the grey stone slates of the roof, at
the chimney stack and some fluffy clouds drifting
across the blue sky.

"Climb!" Naomi gasped, as once more the
head reappeared.

"Oh – my – go-oodness!" Zeta cried. What was
it? Was she dreaming?

Gordon the goat had scaled the heights. He was
perched on the ridge of the roof looking down on
the farmyard.

"He'll fall!" Naomi breathed, clutching Zeta's
arm. "Oh Zeta, he'll kill himself!"

Gordon picked his way along the ridge regardless.

"C'mon!" Zeta cried, dragging Naomi across the yard towards the blacksmith's white van.

"Miss, Miss!" The whole class turned round. Even Pete stopped being cheesy.

Shane jabbed Callum in the ribs one last time. "Look up there!" he warned.

Callum squinted against the sun. He saw a blurred shape trotting along the roof, throwing back its head and opening its mouth wide.

"Gordon!"

"Miss, the goat's escaped from the field!" Zeta yelled. Wow, was it cool to be the bearer of bad news! "It's on the roof! It's gonna fall and kill itself!"

Gordon let out a mighty bleat that split the air.

"Uh-oh, problem!" Shane mouthed.

But Callum ignored him. "How did that happen?" he asked in a loud, innocent voice. "Last time we saw Gordon he was safely locked up in his field!"

5 Who Let the Goat Out?

"Blaaah-blaaah!" Gordon set up a loud, mad bleating. He looked down on the panic in the yard below.

"It's okay, goats can climb mountains," Pete said, to calm the shrieking kids. "They don't fall off even the narrowest ledges. Gordon is going to be fine!"

"Blaaah!" Gordon bleated.

"How did he get out?" Miss Hallam asked.

"I guess someone left the gate open," was Pete's reply.

Zeta shot Callum a sharp look. Hmm, interesting!

"Who was last out of the field?" the stable girl, Hayley, asked. She'd arrived with a long rope, ready to lasso Gordon and bring him down.

Callum swallowed hard. He wished Zeta would stop staring at him. "That'd be the blacksmith," he pointed out. "He had to fetch Dolly, didn't he?"

Shane's grin showed that he admired Callum's quick thinking.

Hmm. Zeta fixed her gaze on Callum's pongy trainers, sure that he knew more than he was saying.

"I didn't even see any goat," the blacksmith grunted, crossly clanging his tools into a metal box and getting ready to leave.

Cheesy Pete stepped in quickly. "It's okay, Frank, no one's blaming you. The point is, Gordon's done this sort of thing before, and he's a devil to catch!"

"Blaaah!" Gordon skipped and hopped along the ridge of the barn roof on dainty feet, reached the chimney stack, then promptly disappeared behind it.

"Ooo-oooh!" the kids gasped. "Where is he? Did he fall off?"

Ten seconds later, Gordon popped his head out from behind the stack. "Hah, fooled you!"

7JH breathed again.

"Tell you what," Pete said, taking Miss Hallam to one

side. "That goat's never going to come down while this lot are 'oohing' and 'aahing'. Why don't you take them down to the river for lunch?"

Hastily she agreed. "Henry and Shane, lead the way to the river!" she ordered. "It's time for lunch!"

"Aah Miss, can't we stay and see what happens?" Shane protested, feeling that this was by far the most interesting part of the day. Goat on roof. Big drop to the ground. Possible splatted goat. Major action. Wicked!

"No we cannot!" Mrs Wilks took control. "Naomi, Zeta, Zoey, come along. Callum, keep up!"

Reluctantly the gaggle of kids made their way out of the farmyard, leaving Pete to play the hero and rescue the goat.

"Where's my sarnies?"

"Who ate my crisps?"

"Ergh, mine are all squashed!"

Lunch boxes were opened, their contents scoffed or fed to the ducks. Shane and Callum went to skim pebbles at the water's edge.

"Five!" Shane claimed on his first attempt. "Did you see it? It bounced five times!"

Callum flipped his stone. "Seven!" he claimed.

The two boys scuffled for the best flat pebbles, while the girls looked on.

"I bet Callum McCoodle was the one who let Gordon out," Zeta murmured, idly stuffing her apple and half a banana into her pocket so she could feed them to the donkeys later.

"How much?" Zoey asked.

"50p."

"You're on!" Zoey said.

For a while they sat and watched ducks flying low above the river, and listened to the gentle murmur of running water.

"Callum and Shane, stop throwing stones!" Miss Hallam noticed them for the first time.

"Aah, Miss!" they complained, scrunching over

the pebbles and slumping down on the grass with the others.

"Boring!" Callum grumbled after five seconds.

"I wonder if they've nabbed the goat yet?" Shane mumbled.

"Oh yeah – Gordon!" Callum had almost forgotten about him in the excitement of skimming stones. But come to think of it, it might be interesting to find out. "Bet you a fiver I can rescue him if he's still on that roof!" he told Shane.

"You're on," Shane agreed. "Dream on, McCoodle!"

Silently Callum rolled down the grassy bank onto the pebble beach, where he was out of sight. Then he wriggled along on his belly, commando-style. He reached a prickly holly bush and paused.

Only Zeta had seen Callum vanish. "Can you believe that?" she hissed.

Naomi and Zoey lay back on the grass in the sun.

Zeta concentrated on which way Callum was going; he was out from behind the bush and heading up to the farm behind their backs. She was about to tell on him, when she thought of something much more interesting to do. She went up to the teacher with a brilliant excuse. "Miss, my mum told me not to stay out in the sun without my sun cream on. The thing is, I've left it on the bus!"

Miss Hallam brushed crumbs off her trousers then delved into her bag. "You can borrow mine," she offered.

"No, Miss. Mine's special. Mum says I've got delicate skin."

The teacher squinted dubiously at Zeta's smooth, tanned face.

"Honest, Miss. I have to use this special stuff. My mum'll kill me if I don't. Can I go and fetch it?"

Shaking her head and sighing, Miss Hallam was forced to give in. "Don't be long," she instructed. "In fact, you can meet us in the farmyard. It's time for us all to pack up here and walk back."

Zeta nodded. Just time then to run ahead, track Callum down and catch him doing something bad, like letting more animals out of fields. She shot off up the grass after him.

And McCoodle slips by the defence. He stays onside. And now it's just him and the goalie ...

Callum sneaked by the field with the lambs. He could hear the pigs snorting in their sties. Wow, Gordon was still prancing about on the roof, laughing at Hayley and Pete's feeble attempts to coax him down.

"The trouble is, every time I climb up there, he skitters off down the other side," Hayley muttered.

"That's because he can see your rope,'" Callum thought. "And rope equals being caught and chucked back in the boring field!" This goat was clever. He worked things out. "But," Callum thought, "if you tried food to tempt him down, that would be a different story." It was obvious; the way to a goat's heart was through his stomach!

"Blaaah!" Gordon screeched from the top of the roof.

Food? Callum searched his pockets, but found only empty wrappers. What did goats eat anyway? Probably hay, like horses. Seizing a handful from a bale stacked inside the barn door, he stuffed it into his pocket.

"Here I come!" Callum said to himself. Anything Pete and Hayley did, he could do better. Anyhow, he'd bet Shane a fiver that he could get that goat down!

And so, without a thought for his own safety, Callum McCoodle, superhero, hoisted himself up a wonky drainpipe onto the roof of the barn.

6 Spiderman!

"Callum, come down!" Zeta hissed. She'd trailed him up from the river, seen him grab the bunch of straw and stick it in his pocket. But she hadn't been close enough to stop him from climbing the drainpipe.

He looked down. "Whoa – no, don't do that!" Dizzily he clutched the pipe and took a deep breath. There was five pounds resting on this.

"You'll break your neck!" Zeta warned.

"Get lost!" he told her. "I'm gonna tempt Gordon off the roof with some nice chewy hay."

"That's not hay, stupid. It's straw!" Zeta pointed out.

"How d'you know?"

"Any idiot can tell the difference between straw and hay."

Clinging to the wobbly pipe, Callum was

beginning to realise that he'd overlooked his fear of heights.

The sound of their excited voices drew Pete and Hayley around the corner. "Hey, come down!" Pete ordered in a strangled voice when he spotted Callum. "That drainpipe's not safe!"

Callum clung on. He looked up at the roof, then down at the ground. "Whoa!" His head spun and his mouth went dry. And now the goat was peering down, having a good laugh. It poked its big head over the edge of the roof and gave a loud snicker.

Zeta scoffed from ground level. "McCoodle-doodle, Mc-Coodle-don't!"

"Stay exactly where you are," Hayley told Callum, rushing off to bring a long ladder which she could rest on the wall alongside the drainpipe. "Now step sideways onto the ladder," she instructed.

Callum's legs wobbled. He closed his eyes and took the sideways step.

"Look at Callum!" Zeta called out to Miss Hallam, Mrs Wilks and the rest of the class, who had just arrived in the farmyard. "He thinks he's Spiderman!"

Miss Hallam froze at the sight of Callum on the ladder. "Please tell me this isn't really happening!" she said in a weak voice.

"It's okay, everything's under control," Pete assured her.

"Steady now," Hayley told Callum. "I'm holding the ladder. All you have to do is make your way slowly down."

Gradually, step-by-step, Callum reached the ground. "I'd have got up there and rescued that goat if you hadn't dobbed me in!" he told Zeta to cover up his shame.

"Yeah!" she snorted. "You were rubbish, Callum, and you know it."

There was no time to argue, though, since this was the moment Gordon chose to make his own move.

Bored with being on the roof and probably hungry, the goat took a run along the ridge, veered sideways down the slates, reached the edge and launched

himself into midair. He landed safely in a trailer piled high with horse manure.

"Ooh! Aah! Wow! Ergh!" the kids cried.

Then Gordon leaped clear and was amongst them; smelling bad, ducking and diving, swerving around anyone who stood in his way.

"Don't panic!" Pete shouted, but it was Hayley with her lasso who tried to stop Gordon from charging straight at Miss Hallam.

"Watch out, Miss!" Zeta cried. She'd spotted the evil look in Gordon's green eye as he'd lowered his head.

The teacher turned and saw the goat charge. She yelped and looked round frantically.

Whoosh! Hayley threw the lasso. It landed uselessly on the ground.

"Ooh! Aah!" cried 7JH.

Their teacher vaulted the pigsty barrier and came face to face with Miss Piggy. Big fat Miss Piggy with seven little piglets. Big, fat, angry Miss Piggy. Her heart sank.

Meanwhile, Gordon wasn't going to let a metre-high fence stand in his way. Oh no! He simply jumped it and joined Miss Piggy, the piglets and Miss Hallam in the pen.

Zeta and Callum raced to take a look. They saw their wimpy teacher hemmed in against the

wall by Miss Piggy and Gordon. Miss Hallam was a gibbering wreck.

"She's lost it!" Callum muttered.

"Big time," Zeta agreed.

"Help!" Miss Hallam cried.

The little pigs squealed and ran everywhere.

"Take this!" Zeta told Callum, handing him the spare apple leftover from her lunch. Then she held up the half-eaten banana as if it was a hand grenade. "We're going in!" she told him.

"You're nuts!" he spluttered.

"Are you coming, or what?" she challenged, climbing the barrier before anyone could stop her.

Callum held back. Gordon's horns looked seriously sharp and Miss Piggy was big enough to steamroller them to a pulp. But there again, he had his reputation to think about – a reputation which was definitely dinted by the drainpipe episode. So he told Zeta to toss him the apple and followed her into the sty.

"Come back, you two!" Cheesy Pete cried, to no avail.

Gordon still had the teacher in his sights. He stood, head down, terrifying the life out of her. Meanwhile, Miss Piggy, the pig mountain, stood guard.

"Here, nice piggy-wiggy!" Zeta held out her banana.

Miss Piggy wiggled her wide snout. "Food – yum!"

"Here, Gordon – lovely apple!" Callum coaxed.

The goat wrinkled his nose. "Food!" Now it was a choice between his stomach and terrorising a teacher. Which should he do?

"Help!" Miss Hallam cried faintly.

"Chomp!" Miss Piggy snaffled the banana.

"Crunch!" Gordon's teeth sank into the crisp apple.

"C'mon, Miss!"

While the animals were busy eating, Callum darted between them and grabbed the teacher's hand. He hauled her through the narrow gap and through the gate that Zeta held open.

"Cool!" the kids cried. "Wicked! Let's hear it for Callum and Zeta!"

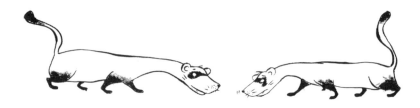

7 A Ferret Called Callum

Cheesy Pete decided to name two ferrets after
Zeta and Callum.

"It's our way of saying thank you," he
explained. "Without them, your lovely Miss
Hallam could have had a nasty accident."

"Cool!" Zeta stroked her furry ferret. "Can I
come and walk Zeta again?" she asked.

"Whenever you want," Pete assured her.

Callum wasn't sure about his namesake.
Callum the ferret looked a bit sly and, well,
ferrety for his liking. "Does he bite?" he asked.

"Not if you take care how you handle him,"
Hayley replied.

Callum had a quick stroke and walked away. So
now there was a ferret called Callum at Low Hall
Farm. That was quite cool, actually. Yeah, well cool.

Then Miss Hallam and Mrs Wilks said it was
time to pile back onto the bus.

"Beep-beep!" Callum roared up the steps and blared in the snoozing driver's ear.

"Bags me the front seat!" Zeta shoved her way to the head of the queue.

Pete and Miss Hallam watched the scrum.

She smiled shyly. "Thank you for putting up with this little lot – er – Pete."

"Erm – er – I was wondering if I could take you out to dinner tomorrow," the manager murmured.

"Ergh, cringe!" Zoey overheard and shot onto the bus to pass on the news. "Miss has pulled!" she screeched above the racket. "Honest, she has. I'm not kidding!"

"I'm starving!" Zeta moaned. She went down the aisle, asking, "Has anyone got any food?"

"Get lost!" Callum told her when she got to him.

"That's not very nice!" Zeta retorted. "After I kept quiet about you letting Gordon out!"

Callum sat up straight with a look of wide-eyed innocence. "What? Who, me?"

"Muck on the trainers!" Zeta pointed out, stony-faced. "So don't deny it."

There was a long silence between them, then Callum's face cracked into a grin. "It was wicked though, wasn't it?"

"Yeah, wild," she grinned back. "Zoey, you owe me 50p!" she yelled down the bus.

"And you owe me a fiver," Callum told Shane.

"What for?" Shane challenged.

Callum squared up for a fight. "For catching Gordon!"

"No, that was for getting him to come down from the roof. And you never did that," his mate argued.

"Did!"

"Didn't!"

"Did!"

"Yeah, he did!" Zeta joined in. Sticking up for

Callum was a first. But she did her maths and saw how far five pounds divided by two would go. "I was there, Shane, and Callum definitely did scare Gordon into coming down!"

Shane frowned. A fiver was a lot of money. "No, he didn't!" he said again.

This argument was set to run and run, all the way up the lane, along the winding country roads, back into town after what had, after all, been a perfect day.

"Sit down at the back!" Miss Hallam screeched. "Fasten your seat belts. Here we go!"